BestBooks 6th   12/60

6/08

E
FICTION
LIN

NORTH COUNTRY SPRING

Reeve Lindbergh

Paintings by Liz Sivertson

Houghton Mifflin Company
Boston 1997

All over the north, a new voice is heard,
Deep as the river and high as a bird,
Fresh as the meadow and strong as a tree;
It calls over and over, *Come! Listen to me!*

Come out, calls the voice, whoever you are.
Come out with the dawn and the morning star.

Come out in the sun as it melts the snows.
Come out with the brook as it overflows.

Spread out, it sings to the trees. *Be first.*
Fill with sweet sap till your leaf-buds burst.

Take wing, wild geese, calls the voice. *Fly high!*
Soar a hundred miles through an April sky.

Amble out, sniff the air, it says next to the bear.
Let your brown cubs tumble everywhere.

Step out, do not fear, calls the voice to the deer.
Come and nibble the new green grasses here.

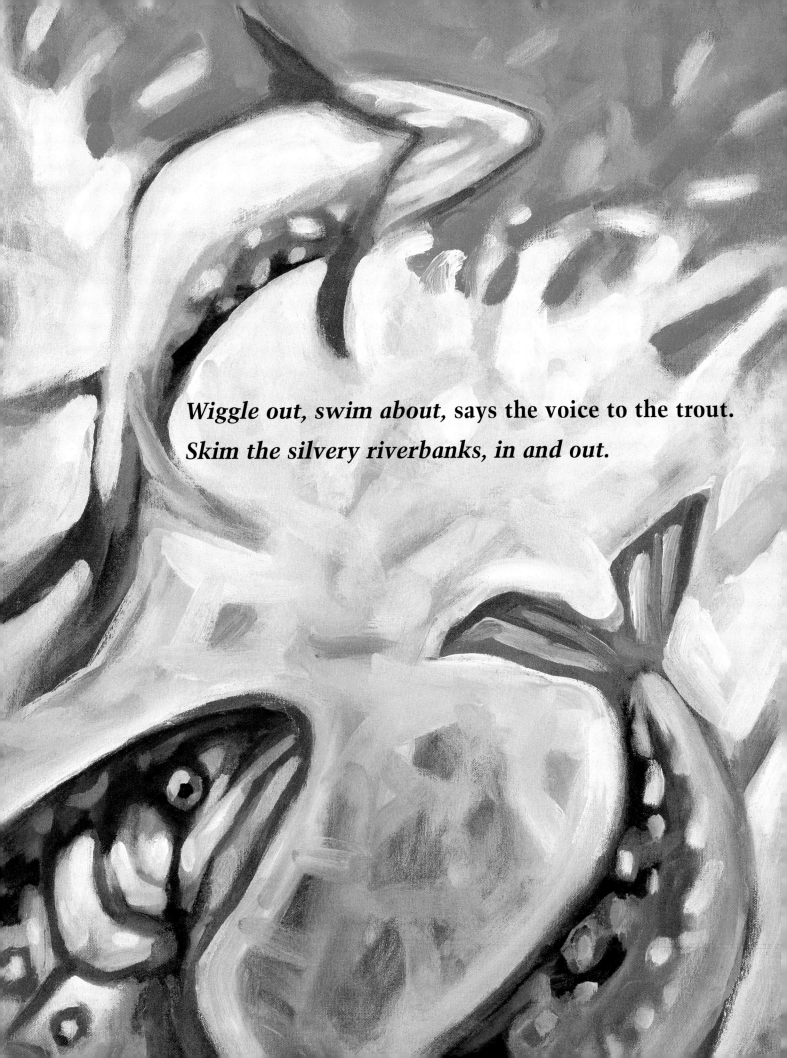

Wiggle out, swim about, says the voice to the trout.
Skim the silvery riverbanks, in and out.

Leap in, little peepers, to the pond and bring
Your frog-pond heart-throb tune to sing.

Glide down, wild duck, to the marsh and rest.

Hide a clutch of eggs in a wetland nest.

Strut out, tall moose, from your stand of spruce.
Walk around, feel the ground, let your bones get loose.

Slip in, sleek otters, from the river's side.
Splash and play all day, make a big mud slide.

Come out in the daytime, come out in the night.
Come out with the new moon, silent and bright.

Fly out, blinking owl, says the voice. Fly free!
Float over the shadowy woods with me.

Skitter out, little mice, but take care — be wise!

The dark has more than a thousand eyes.

Swoop out, swift bat, flutter fast, flitter-flit.
Snatch a moth on the wing; make a meal of it.

Shuffle out, slow skunk, snuffle here, snuffle there.
Grub for bugs and slugs; food is everywhere.

Lope out, wild wolves, come out and prowl.
It's a fine shiny night for a yip and a howl.

Come out, calls the voice, *whoever you are.*
Come out in the dark, with the dancing stars.
Come, children; come, parents; come, grandparents, too.
Come out, *hear the voice that is calling to you.*

I am the breeze that is warming the land,
The fast-flowing river that washes your hand,

The green grass at your feet, the white clouds flying high,
The seeds in the ground and the wings in the sky.

I am the ducklings that hatch in the nest,
The rain in the forest, the wind from the west,

The violets in meadows
when snow is all gone,

The bear cub,
the fox kit,
the white-spotted fawn.

I am the voice inside every new thing,

The song of beginnings,

The song of spring!

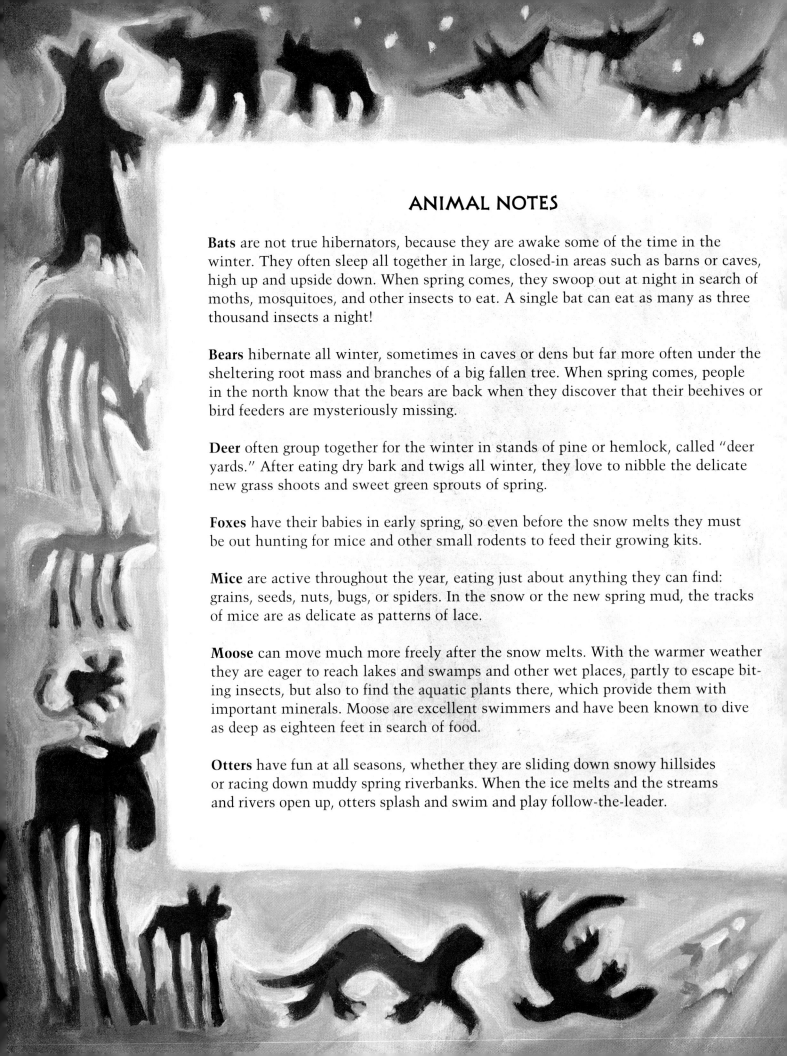

ANIMAL NOTES

Bats are not true hibernators, because they are awake some of the time in the winter. They often sleep all together in large, closed-in areas such as barns or caves, high up and upside down. When spring comes, they swoop out at night in search of moths, mosquitoes, and other insects to eat. A single bat can eat as many as three thousand insects a night!

Bears hibernate all winter, sometimes in caves or dens but far more often under the sheltering root mass and branches of a big fallen tree. When spring comes, people in the north know that the bears are back when they discover that their beehives or bird feeders are mysteriously missing.

Deer often group together for the winter in stands of pine or hemlock, called "deer yards." After eating dry bark and twigs all winter, they love to nibble the delicate new grass shoots and sweet green sprouts of spring.

Foxes have their babies in early spring, so even before the snow melts they must be out hunting for mice and other small rodents to feed their growing kits.

Mice are active throughout the year, eating just about anything they can find: grains, seeds, nuts, bugs, or spiders. In the snow or the new spring mud, the tracks of mice are as delicate as patterns of lace.

Moose can move much more freely after the snow melts. With the warmer weather they are eager to reach lakes and swamps and other wet places, partly to escape biting insects, but also to find the aquatic plants there, which provide them with important minerals. Moose are excellent swimmers and have been known to dive as deep as eighteen feet in search of food.

Otters have fun at all seasons, whether they are sliding down snowy hillsides or racing down muddy spring riverbanks. When the ice melts and the streams and rivers open up, otters splash and swim and play follow-the-leader.

Owls are generally nocturnal; throughout the year they fly over night-dark fields and woods in search of mice and other small animals to pounce upon. Owls are very busy in the spring, because they lay their eggs and have their hatchlings earlier than many other birds do.

Peepers are very small frogs, about the size of an adult's thumbnail. Their happy trilling song fills the air on spring evenings. They sound like a chorus celebrating the warm weather and fresh air after a long winter spent deep and dark in the mud at the edge of the pond.

Ravens cruise the skies all year round looking for food, circling and soaring over the countryside even on the most bitter of winter days. When the snow melts in spring, they are like treasure hunters, looking for whatever shows up on the ground.

Skunks hibernate in burrows underground for most of the winter, but as soon as the ground thaws, they begin to come out to hunt for small grubs and insects.

Trout spend the winter at the bottoms of the rivers, not doing much at all. They are cold-blooded and so can stay alive under freezing conditions because their body processes slow down as the temperature drops. When the ice melts and the water starts to flow more swiftly, they instinctively leap up toward the sunlight to catch newly hatched insects, then fall back to join the stream again.

Wild ducks and **geese** fly back north in early spring, after spending the winter in coastal marshes, along unfrozen shorelines of the Great Lakes, or in sheltered southern waterways. They sometimes fly overhead in flocks of a hundred or more, with high, honking noises heralding their return.

Wolves do not hibernate, because their thick fur keeps them warm all winter. In the spring, they begin to lose their winter fur, so their coats may look rough and patchy. Wolves love to dig in the dirt, especially when the snow and ice have melted and the soil is loose and free again.

For Margot —R.L.

For Chris and Annie.
Special thanks to Joyce for reminding me
that spring would eventually come. —L.S.

The text of this book is set in Trump Medieval.
The illustrations are acrylic, reproduced in full color.

For information about this and other Houghton Mifflin trade and reference
books and multimedia products, visit The Bookstore at Houghton Mifflin
on the World Wide Web at http://www.hmco.com/trade/.

Manufactured in the United States of America
BVG 10 9 8 7 6 5 4 3 2 1

Library of Congress Cataloging-in-Publication Data
Lindbergh, Reeve.
North country spring / written by Reeve Lindbergh ; paintings by Liz Sivertson. — 1st ed.
p. cm.
Summary: Rhyming verse and illustrations describe the arrival of
spring in the north. Includes section with facts about animal behavior.
ISBN 0-395-82819-8 [1. Spring — Fiction. 2. Animals — Fiction. 3. Stories in rhyme.]
I. Sivertson, Liz, ill. II. Title. PZ8.3.L6148No 1997 [E] — dc20 95-52366 CIP AC